Bounds

Death to Romeo

*Dedicated to those who seek the truth,
dedicated to those who never tire
in the search for justice,
dedicated to those who are not
deterred by illusion.*

PrisonersOfSilence.org

Katia Anedda

Bounds – Death to Romeo

ISBN - 978-1-257-11201-2

1) **True crime**   2) **Carlo Parlanti**   3) **Rebecca White**

Although this is a work of fiction, the names, characters, places and incidents are real and taken directly from the documentation of the controversial case "The People Vs. Carlo Parlanti".

The entire documentation is published on the web site

http://www.ThePeopleVsCarloParlanti.com

Prisoners of Silence

C.F. 93072830388

Association to safeguard the rights of Italians held in foreign prisons

http://www.PrisonersOfSilence.org

E-mail: info@prisonersofsilence.org

Table of Contents

Bounds

Death to Romeo

Premise of the play

In one act, "Bounds" is the theatrical representation of the accusations included in the case "The People of the state of California Vs. Carlo Parlanti".

Carlo Parlanti, an Information Technology Manager working in California for Dole, was accused of serious charges involving actions which criminologists and experts have declared impossible.

Carlo was essentially kidnapped from Europe, a crime which, as of October 2009, the U.S. District Attorney's Office has no intention of prosecuting.

For six years, since July 2004, following his arrest in Germany, his life long companion, Katia Anedda, along with his family, have relentlessly sought to capture the attention of the public and world media.

While they have received much in the way of positive feedback, there have been many more disillusionments.

In 2008, "Prisoners of Silence" was founded when six women, meeting together to discuss the injustices of Carlo's case, decided there was a need for a non profit organization which would safeguard the rights of Italians being held in foreign prisons: for all the Carlo Parlantis who do not have a Katia Anedda to support them.

All documentation relating to Carlo Parlanti's case has been published from the very beginning and is available by visiting: www.thepeoplevscarloparlanti.com

The organization faces all of the challenges associated with contacting and communicating with officials of foreign countries and needs your help because:

"No man is an island, entire of itself; every man is a piece of the continent, a part of the main. If a clod be washed away by the sea, Europe is the less, as well as if a promontory were, as well as if a manor of thy friend's or of thine own were. Any man's death diminishes me, because I am involved in mankind; and therefore never send to know for whom the bell tolls; it tolls for thee..."

John Donne

Act one

Scene I - A living room

[A living room in an apartment, in perfect order. A baker's rack style bookcase is located 3 feet Stage Right from the entrance to the room at center stage up; it acts as a screen between the entrance door and the room. On the ground near the bookcase is a bag and two boxes. Rebecca is on her knees in front of one of the boxes. She looks up to the bookcase and her attention is grabbed by one of the books on the shelf of the case. It is in Italian. She flips idly through a few pages and then discards it on the floor.]

Rebecca - *[Highly agitated, to self]* You'll see... you'll see. I'll find it. I know it's around here, it was right here in the middle of these books. *[Continues looking for the book, flipping pages. Finally she finds the book she's looking for]* Here it is! What did I tell you? *[She reads]* "... One cannot love running water and lock it up in a drawer. I will always be your best friend." See? She says she's his "best friend". But really... she loves him and she's saying he's some kind of free spirit that can't be confined.

[A female character enters stage left, her face expressionless. She bends and whispers in her ear]

Woman - Basically, "I'm leaving you because I love you too much..." *[She bursts into derisive laughter]* The same old bullshit!

Rebecca - *[Turns, frightened, almost paranoid, toward the woman; then*

---

disgustedly] You think so?

Woman - You don't?

Rebecca - No.

Woman - I do.

Rebecca - I'll prove it. *[shakes the book]* He even translated the dedication! He translated it! He kept the book!

Woman - Why should he throw it away? You still keep your diaries from high school, all those "Luv U's", the little hearts, "He's hot"...

Rebecca - It's totally different!

Woman - It's the same.

Rebecca - We're not in high school anymore.

Woman - Exactly. Why can't you act like an adult?

[Pause]

Woman - So that's why you're leaving, and the mad-dog attitude? That's why? The dedications... the memories... the women? After a year you should know how he is. He would never throw out a book... Especially since it's from her? She was there before you, she's there now, she's gonna be there forever. Other women come and go, but

---

she always remains *[Laughs again]*. And the reason she does is because... how was that? She doesn't "lock up running water in a drawer". *[Another laugh, louder this time]* You don't learn, do you, my dear? You want to leave? Fine, but be honest about it. What do you plan on doing?

Rebecca - *[Whispering]* He's the one that wants it.

[A pause while Rebecca moves the boxes toward the door]

Rebecca - He had a lot of women.

Woman - Well, you would have had a lot of men, too... if you could have.

Rebecca - What's that suppose to mean?

Woman - Nothing. It doesn't mean anything. What do you think having a lot of women is supposed to mean?!

Rebecca - But I've never done with anybody else what I've done with him. He made me discover sex... love... *[changing tone]* and maybe he did that for them, too? If it was love for me, what was it for him? And for those other women? And what about "Miss Running Water"? And now this new one... the one he's got in Mississippi?

Woman - *[A wry smile]* You wanted him all to yourself? I think "Miss Running Water" pretty well saw through him, dear. *[Another irritating laugh]* You wanted him to be all for yourself. That's not love. You're sick.

Rebecca - *[Shrieking]* Stop it! I'm not crazy!

Woman - You said it, not me. *[whispering]* I only said "sick".

[Pause]

Woman - Come on. What's it going to be? You can talk to me. So you like being bound, blindfolded and spanked? You asked him to, remember?

Rebecca - But... I... I... No, wait... He liked it. I asked him to because he liked it!! Stop it! I'm not like that! He wanted it! *[She doubles up into nearly a fetal position, sobbing]*

Woman - Him, him, him. He only does what you like. You still don't get it, do you? He comes when he feels you coming thanks to him. And you, poor little stupid, still don't understand. You can't stand that somebody else understands him, that he's got someone else... that sooner or later, he's going back to "Miss Running Water".

Rebecca - *[Covering her ears]* Why did you come here? Go away!

Woman - *[Low tone]* You can cover your ears all you want. You know that you're hearing me no matter what.

Rebecca - Yes, I hear you, I hear you!

[Pause]

Woman - You know, I think it's time to leave.

Rebecca - *[Collecting herself]* You're right. We need to go report him to the police.

Woman - Report him? For what?

Rebecca - He's violent... He may become dangerous... He may become violent.

Woman - He's violent or he "may" become violent? Make up your mind.

Rebecca - Oh, stop nit-picking at everything I say.

Woman - If you're going to report him, you've got to be precise.

Rebecca - He drinks. When he drinks, he gets violent.

Woman - Oh my God! He drinks!... Like everybody that drinks... Violence... I don't remember any violence. I don't know if you can make that one stick. Even your husband... he was violent too, right? Change the script, dear.

Rebecca - My husband... that was in Texas. Nobody knows about that. Besides... he even admitted to it. And why shouldn't it stick? *[Shows fingers close]* It was this far from working with you, wasn't it? You said yourself that he was violent. This time, it's going to ruin him. He's got priors.

Woman - But we know. We know the truth. I'm me, you're you... *[Giving in]* oh, alright. Maybe it could stick. But I'm telling you, you're going to have to be more precise.

[Pause. Woman laughs to herself and Rebecca sees her]

Woman - I suppose you could say "he forced me" or "he threatened me" or that you couldn't talk. Write this down Rebecca, or you're going to forget this stuff. It's easy to forget lies. *[Pause]* A calendar... you need a calendar. You're going to need something like a diary too. If you're going to report him, you'd better be convincing. This is a much better idea than you think, girl. If you handle this right you're going to come out with free medical right? Because... and correct me if I'm wrong... you're without insurance right now, aren't you?

Rebecca - Right. What am I supposed to do about my drugs? They're expensive. And what if I have to move out?

Woman - You need to be convincing. Don't mention the drugs. That's a real problem.

Rebecca - I'm not stupid, don't call me stupid, not you, too. I'm going to be convincing. A woman is always convincing, as long as she says it with feeling. Anyway, he's not even American. I am, and I'm not stupid.

[Pause]

Woman - Ok. Tell me, then. Convince me. Convince me, too.

Rebecca - It... it was two weeks ago. Let's see... today's the 18th. Yes. *[Counting on fingers]* July 18th. Yes, it was the 6th. The 6th of July. It was a Saturday... A Saturday. He was working at the computer, then something went wrong. We bought groceries, and afterwards he was at the computer and frustrated and I... I wanted to do something for him, he looked at me all angry... like it was my fault that something went wrong... he was talking that afternoon to her... on the phone... no, I can't say that! There's no "her". He just said to me "get lost. Get out of my sight." I didn't think... I thought he meant to get out of his office and go to the bedroom or something.

Woman - Then?

Rebecca - *[Shrug]* I went to bed. After about 10 minutes he comes in and says "you didn't hear me. I told you to get lost. Like in 'get out of my house and don't come back'." He grabbed me... hard... by my arm and threw me on the floor... he dragged me... he put his hand under my chin... he put his hips against mine and then he banged me ten times... no thirty... yes, thirty times, against the wall right by the front door. *[Moves around, almost like miming or reenacting. She nears the drywall by the door and points]* Here. Yes. Here. *[To herself]* Yes, that's good. That's very good. Keep going, Rebecca.

Woman - Go on. So this is the story you're going to use? It's not working. You need to prepare. This one's not cutting it.

Rebecca - Yes it does! It does stand up! I'll come up with the rest of it. He shouldn't ever do what he did to me to anyone else.

[Pause. Woman stands in silence. Rebecca regards Woman for a moment]

Woman - Are you sure you want to do this?

Rebecca - I have to do it. He cannot... he cannot be with another woman.

Woman - So this is… what you can't stand, isn't it?

Rebecca - Stop! Now, you shut up!

[Pause. Rebecca picks up the remaining scattered books and returns them to the bookcase]

Woman - Are we gonna miss him? *[No answer from Rebecca]* Does he have another one?

[Silence. Rebecca goes toward the door. Light fades, leaving only one ray of light on the two women, who stand in the center of the room]

Woman - Are you sure he's dangerous?

[Dark]

[End of Scene I]

Silence is a barrier that separates more than barbed wire and hurts more than torture

Scene II - Fullerton's Office

[An office. A desk (on which is a PC, pens and folders) is at stage left. Two chairs are in front of the desk. On the wall is a portrait of the President and the District Attorney. On either side is alternately a California State flag and an American flag. Sgt. Fullerton stands in front of the desk. Sgt. Reilly is seated behind the desk. Fullerton hands a sheaf of documents to Reilly, who begins to punch data into the keyboard, researching something. Fullerton paces, somewhat impatiently until Reilly exhales with finality at having found what he has been looking for. Both men appear relieved and satisfied.]

Fullerton - That's it for today.

Reilly - Thank God.

[Long Pause]

Fullerton - Okay Jane's out at her girl's tonight. I can take it easy

Reilly - Want to grab a beer at the end of the shift? It's on me.

Fullerton - You bet. Thanks.

[Pause. Keller enters stage left with Rebecca and leads her to one of the chairs.]

[Rebecca looks very upset, shaken. She is agitated. The two officers are taken aback by the sudden appearance of Rebecca and exchange looks with Keller inquisitively, expectantly.]

Keller - *[To Rebecca]* This is Sgt. Fullerton and this is Sgt. Reilly, Rebecca. Why don't you tell them what's happened... as best you can remember.

Fullerton - *[Taken by surprise]* Good evening Miss. How can I help you?

Rebecca – I... I need to report... He... He hurt me... He's got to be stopped...

Fullerton - Calm down, Miss. Who's "he"? Who do you mean? How did "he" hurt you?

Rebecca - My... Carlo... My boyfriend... He was upset with me because of my mother and my daughter... then he drank... He was drinking... He drinks when he's stressed, you know... He's developing a program, a computer program, and it doesn't work...

Fullerton - Okay, Miss, Officer Keller is going to take you into the interview room. I'm going to join you in a minute as soon as I can find a recorder and then you can tell me everything in detail from the beginning.

[Pause. The four go to the exit. Room goes black, only shadows of Rebecca and Officers are visible. They exit the door.]

[End of Scene II]

Scene III - Interview Room

[An interview room. A table is at stage center with three chairs around the table. Rebecca is seated down at stage center. Fullerton enters from stage left and sits at the down stage end of the table. He shoots Reilly, who stands not far from Fullerton, a worried look.]

Fullerton - Well Miss... let's begin. Could you please tell us clearly who you are and what your boyfriend did to you?

Rebecca - *[Trying to calm herself, but speaking rapidly, tensely]* Yes... my name is... Rebecca White. His name is Carlo Parlanti. I met him in Monterey over a year ago. After that his company, Dole, offered him a job down here in Westlake and I came with him. We've been living together for eight, nine... yes, nine months. *[Pause]* On July 6th Saturday, it was Saturday... he was working at his computer and then something went wrong. We bought groceries. My mother and my daughter... they came to visit me. They left early. He was at his computer and he was getting frustrated and I... I wanted to do something for him, he looked at me angry, he drank a two liter bottle of wine. Then he sent me to buy another two liters. As if it was my fault something was wrong with his program... it was night, no, it wasn't dark yet. Maybe it was six or seven.

Fullerton - *[Perplexed, to Rebecca]* And you? You went to buy it?

Rebecca - Yes. I went to Walmart. It's near our apartment. Then I went back home. He'd gotten started on the second bottle, he told me "Get lost. Get out of my sight." I didn't think... I thought he meant for me to leave his study and go to the bedroom. After ten minutes he came in and told me: "You don't understand. I meant for you to get out of my house. Get out and don't ever come back." He grabbed my arm and threw me to the floor. He dragged me... he put his hand under my jaw. His hips pressed into mine and he banged me many times against the wall at the entrance and then against the bulletin board hanging between the two doors. He squeezed my neck very hard.

Reilly - It's alright. It's alright Miss... Try to calm down... can you wait just a second? Just a second... I need to talk to my partner.

[Pause. Reilly turns off the recorder and pulls Fullerton to the side, away from Rebecca]

Fullerton - *[Whispering]* So... that was "it for today", huh? I think we need to get everybody in here. They're not going to want to miss this one. It's quite a tragedy.

Reilly - Come on, Mark. That's the last thing we need. Do we have time to waste on this? If this is just a domestic violence, lets get the report, go grab this Mexican boyfriend or whatever, make him cool his heels in the tank and go get our beer for Pete's sake.

Fullerton - He's not Mexican. I think he's Italian. This isn't making sense. Tell you what: go back to the office, do a quick search on the guy and see if anything turns up. *[Reilly leaves, Fullerton returns to Rebecca]* Do you feel like going on, Miss?

[Pause. Rebecca seems anxious. She looks nervously at the floor, entwining her fingers absently]

Fullerton - Miss... Rebecca... How do you feel? Can I get you something to drink? Maybe we should have a doctor look at you... *[Rebecca Shakes head refusing]* We'll figure all this out... just try to calm down... *[Fullerton waits for Reilly to return]*

Rebecca - No... a doctor... no. It wouldn't prove anything. I've had sex with him since then. I love him. Too much time's already gone by since... since he...

[Pause]

[Reilly returns with a sheaf of papers in his hand]

Reilly - *[Indicating for Fullerton to join him away from the table]* He's an I.T. Manager. Some big fish. Works for Dole. May be a good collar for us. If this guy's got anything to hide, any skeletons, it's definitively a plus as far as the D.A.'s concerned. He's campaigning on a crimes against women platform this election.

Fullerton - Good. So you're a ladder climber after all. Nice one. And if he's not a citizen and she is, it's even nicer.

Reilly - Okay, Mark. On top of everything else... these Italians... they all think they're some kind of Latin lover, all Romeos. Anyway... I've got them doing a full background on this guy next door.

Fullerton - Perfect! Thanks. *[goes back to Rebecca]* Here I am. Back with you. I had something important to ask my partner. I'm going to start the recorder and we can keep going if you feel up to it. We were at the point where you said you went to the bedroom. He had drank a 2 liter bottle of wine and he started the second one, is that right? He asked you to get lost... to get out of his sight. Correct?

Rebecca - *[Nodding nervously]* Correct.

Fullerton - Do you always do what he tells you to?

Silence is a barrier that separates more than barbed wire and hurts more than torture

Rebecca - Yes. Especially when he drinks. He's been violent with me before. *[Pause]* Violent, in fact... when he drinks, only when he drinks. I... I went to bed, but after about ten minutes he came into the bedroom and he told me that I didn't understand. He said "Go ahead, Rebecca, get out of my house. Get out and don't come back." He scared me. I told him that I would have gone and then started getting dressed... As soon as I started getting dressed he got even more angry because I was going to leave. Then he grabbed me... really hard... and banged me against the entrance to the apartment. *[Strangled sob]*

Reilly - *[Aside to Fullerton]* Well... I gotta say... if she was in the bedroom... but her head ended up by the front door getting banged into the wall, she had to have made a pretty big leap. Isn't it more likely she's making this part up? Well... I'm going to go check up on the search results. *[Exits]*

Fullerton – So... he banged you against the bulletin board at the entrance to the apartment.

Rebecca - Yes, I thought he wanted to send me away. Instead... instead, when he saw that I was leaving, he got even more angry. I didn't know what to do anymore... He started to strangle me: the next day my neck was still swollen *[Pause]*. He forced me to my knees. He held me in front of him, I kept quiet... didn't move. Then he started kicking me. Ten kicks on my right rib cage. I couldn't breathe... you know... pain from the broken ribs. Then he grabbed me, taking me by the arm, and put me down on a bean-bag chair. Then he grabbed me by the hair and dragged me into the office. He made me sit on the couch... and then he showed me pictures on the computer.

Fullerton - Pictures? What pictures?

Rebecca - Yes... of women. Bound. Naked. He asked me how I wanted to be bound. I didn't know, I was just scared.

Fullerton - Of course. I understand... *[Rebecca covers her face. Sobs can be heard. Fullerton turns off recording]*

[The room becomes dark, like the conscience of Rebecca White. A ray of light behind her reveals the Woman, expressionless and dispassionate]

Woman - Good, Rebecca. You're learning... You almost don't need me anymore. You're not nearly as stupid as I thought. You're almost convincing.

Rebecca - *[Facing Woman, whispering, careful to not be overheard]* What do you want? I'm not doing anything wrong. Nothing at all. I gave him another chance, but he made me suffer. He dated other women. I gave him a chance to fix everything but he's tired of me. He's in Mississippi now and tonight... he's going to sleep... with... with...

20 Silence is a barrier that separates more than barbed wire and hurts more than torture

Woman - Come on, say the name... it starts with "C"... poor Rebecca. It's not as terrible as that "Miss Running Water"... don't make excuses for yourself... you know how he thinks, how these things go... you knew from the start that he made you no promises.

Rebecca - Stop it! He has to pay for what he's done. He shouldn't do this to other women.

Woman - (sarcastic) Not quite... the correct phrase is actually "he shouldn't be with other women."

Rebecca - Go away! I don't need you for this.

Woman - Of course not, you can destroy lives all by yourself, can't you? *[Moves away but remains on stage, observing]*

[Pause] - [Reilly returns]

Reilly - *[Takes Fullerton aside]* You understand all this, right? The I.T. Manager... the big fish? Well, get this: the guy's got stuff. one DUIs.

Fullerton - Is that a fact? Maybe he was just over the limit. Happens all the time.

Reilly - Yeah, well... [points to the paperwork] he also had some problem with his therapist. A certain Ms. Hollingsworth. Looks like he was fucking her.

Fullerton - This too? For something like that she must have got into trouble... not him. I mean... a doctor... fucking her client?

Reilly - No... no... he went to jail over it. Then he plead-out. Go figure. The guy can't catch a break.

Fullerton - Save the pity…

Reilly - Too bad. Maybe he's talented... anyway, the kid looks real sharp. If the tables were turned, you could believe he was the abused party.

Fullerton - Know what I think? In a little while our shift's over. Even if he's not a US citizen and he's done some stupid things, this woman's not all there, but she is an American citizen; we go pick him up and we make him confess that he put hands on the woman. He pays and he goes on with his life. What's more, the D.A. gets his conviction.

[Pause. The two officers go back to the deposition and the recorder is turned back on]

Fullerton - So, he banged you again? Against the entrance door?

Rebecca - No, not against the door... nearby there's a sort of beam... a column... between the two doors.

Woman - *[Nearing Rebecca, into her ear]* But it's not drywall! That's not believable! He would have cracked your skull against that thing!

Rebecca - *[Whispers, hiding her mouth]* It doesn't matter. They don't know that.

Fullerton - I'm sorry Miss? I missed that. Could you say that again for me?

Rebecca - No... I'm sorry. I was just praying... for strength. *[Gathers herself]* I was just saying that the bulletin board hanging there... the hits were vicious. I had bumps for days. They hurt... he banged me with all his might... I was losing hair by the handful from the back of my head... the nape of my neck... there was so much torn out that the next day it clogged the shower drain.

Reilly - *[Aside]* That's some force... I bet. This isn't some skinny little guy. Forget the bumps for a minute. Did you check out her nape? Look at it. Doesn't look like any is missing at all... unless, of course it magically grew right back. *[talking to Rebecca]* I'm sorry Miss, please go on.

Rebecca - Then... yes. He threw me against the adjacent wall and started hitting me in the face.

Woman - *[Still whispering, again nearing Rebecca]* Oh... great. Just great. That wall is drywall. You do realize that if they go and look it's going to be undamaged. Nothing's broken.

Rebecca - *[Ignoring Woman]* In my face... it was excruciating... my left eye started to swell... he had never been that violent before... never... I was scared.

Fullerton - But... didn't you say before that he had already shown that kind of violence while drinking?

Rebecca - Yes... yes... but he had never been like that before.

Reilly - *[Aside]* I don't know why, but I just don't see it. Oh well, just as long as we get through this and go home.

Rebecca - Believe me... I was scared, I was shaking... I told him I wanted to leave, to let me go... He told me no, he didn't want me to... because, he said, he couldn't stand to be without me. *[Pause]* He started strangling me. Even the next day my neck was still swollen. I lost consciousness and fell to the floor. *[she punctuates her description with a measured sobbing]*

[Fullerton stops the recorder and steps away from the table]

Woman - It's falling apart, girl. It's all falling apart. You're looking insane. First he's throwing you out, then he can't live without you? Make up your mind, woman!

Rebecca - *[Whispering to Woman, almost a hiss]* It's going to work! I'm a woman, and a married one! He's a Romeo and he played me like some...

Woman - He never promised you a thing.

Rebecca - Doesn't matter. I loved him and he hurt me. He made me cry.

Women - You're insane, you know. But, on the bright side, it works in your favor.

Fullerton - *[To Reilly, seeking confirmation]* Are you getting all this?

Reilly - Sure am.

Fullerton - I don't know why, but all this is sounding pretty ambiguous.

Reilly - Sure, Mark, but what do you want to do? Are we going to take the time investigating this stuff? Looks to me like there's an easy way to do it. We go see this guy... no matter what, he's already done some stupid things... *[looks over papers and hands them to Fullerton]*

Fullerton - Bullshit. A couple of beers behind the wheel... *[Pause and scans papers further]* Well, there's also that thing with his therapist, though he's the one filing for damages... anyway, he was fucking her. Either way you cut it, she wasn't very professional. Looks bad.

Reilly - Weird. He got busted? She breaks the law and he does the time? I don't know, Mark. I still think my way is easiest. We go get him, he confesses, he pays, and we go get our beer.

Fullerton - *[Looking at Rebecca from their distance]* Confess? If there's anything to confess at all... did you look at her? Punches... kicks... banging... strangling... but I can't even see a scratch on her.

Reilly - Well it has been a couple of days. Maybe she just now felt up to coming in. Look... she fell for the wrong guy. Same old song and dance, some pizza eating mandolin player. They're all alike, a little passion, a little perversion. I like it. it's more believable like that. *[to self as if trying to convince himself]*

Fullerton - *[Looking doubtful]* Hum... *[Goes to desk and starts recorder]* Excuse me... we were at... you passing out.

Rebecca - Yes... when I woke up I was laying on the floor on my belly. He was on my right, with his knee pressing on my back... here *[indicating on her back]*. Right here.

Silence is a barrier that separates more than barbed wire and hurts more than torture

Fullerton - You couldn't call for help?

Rebecca - I was scared, he kept... he kept strangling me. I couldn't talk... I don't know what happened then. I must have passed out again, because the next thing I remember I was on the other side of the room... and he was still kicking me... and I yelled... at the top of my lungs... the kicks were so hard... I fell, like this... *[Assumes a fetal like, protective folding position]*. I told him he was hurting me.

Reilly - Incredible! *[Aside to Fullerton]* She couldn't talk... then she yelled. If she was yelling at the top of her lungs, someone heard her. They live in an apartment where you can't sneeze without someone hearing you. That shouldn't be hard to verify.

Rebecca - *[Keeps going]* He kept hitting me. I started yelling again, only louder, and he yelled back "stop yelling! Are you trying to get me in trouble?" I... I could barely talk because of the paralysis in my face from his beatings. We were right by the door. The pain in my jaw from his slaps made these shooting stabs. *[Pause, distracted]* Then he dragged me by my left arm and threw me onto a bean-bag chair. You know? One of those chairs with the styrofoam balls inside?

Fullerton - I've seen them, Miss White, do you need a couple of minutes?

Rebecca - Yes, thank you. I'm fine.

[Pause. Fullerton indicates to Reilly water for Rebecca. The two exchange a loaded expression, a mixture of disdain and incredulity of Rebecca]

Woman - You're on thin ice. You're repeating yourself. I told you that you needed to prepare.

Rebecca - I already have experience with this. Shut up. I'm in shock... this is normal... Psychologists know that. I can't be expected to be exact.

[Reilly returns with water and Rebecca resumes after a small sip]

Rebecca - I was nearly blind... I kept telling him. Then he grabbed me by the hair and dragged me through the office door and forced me to sit on the couch. I was so tired. It must have been around midnight.

Reilly - *[To Fullerton, in a whisper]* Wow. Strong guy... after all that wine... 4 liters in 5 hours? According to the charts, he should have been dead. *[Fullerton gestures to Reilly to be quiet]*

Rebecca - He told me that he would never let me go... I was scared... then he said he didn't care what happened to me. He knew he had injured me and that I was going to report him *[Pause]*. He grabbed the phone and shoved it at me and said "here, call 911 and stop this. Report me. Come on" *[Pause]*. I knew if I even touched that phone... I was in so much pain I couldn't even imagine being hit again. I tried to stand up but my ribs were in too much pain. He went to the computer and forced me to look at dirty pictures of women all bound up. Then he said "look... choose which one you want done." He'd tied me up before, so I was scared. *[Pause. Then abruptly, almost screaming]* "I want to go away. Let me go!" *[Pause. Returns to normal tone of voice, conversational]* I begged him, but he wouldn't budge. He grabbed my arm and dragged me into the bedroom and finished undressing me, then... *[Interrupts with sobs]*

Woman - *[Whispering to Rebecca]* Good! Not even I could have done better! But you're getting repetitive. Try to spice it up a little.

Rebecca - He took some of those plastic ties that we use to tie together computer cables out of the closet. He put one on each of my wrists and ankles, as tight as he could. Then he tied my right arm and ankle together, and my left arm and ankle together. He kept tying me up like this for days... four days... yes... until Wednesday.

Fullerton - I'm sorry, I don't understand. He left you that way? Bound? While he was in the house?

Rebecca - No. He was at work during the day. The morning after

---

this happened, he went to work.

Fullerton - The morning after? On a Sunday?

Rebecca - Yes. Yes. Sometimes he works on weekends. And he was also going to the gym. The alarm clock went off at 6:30.

Woman – Uh... rephrase that one. How could you be tied up that way for so long? All day for four days? Think, girl. Couldn't happen.

Fullerton - Night and day... for four days?

Rebecca - No... no... not during the day. During the day I was free. At night he was scared I would try to run away, so he only tied me up at night, you know? During the day I couldn't run away because... he threatened me if I did. *[She stops, silently looking at Fullerton. Pregnant pause]*

[Fullerton reaches for the recorder and purposefully turns it off]

Fullerton - *[Sigh]* Okay, Miss, that's enough. That's fine. Now we're going to fix it all, okay? *[Moves toward Reilly]* So, what do you think?

Reilly - Listen, I didn't understand much of that. I'm thinking revenge. She's got no bruises, no marks... but...

Fullerton - Look, let's start writing up her deposition. We'll tell her she's got to make an appointment to see a doctor. If the exam supports her claim and this guy is guilty of this, we're going to make it stick and he'll pay. Stay here, I'm going to take her to Keller for photos. I'm afraid our shift is going to go into overtime tonight, pal.

Reilly - But the book calls for a medical exam.

Fullerton - Get real. At this hour? With her story? With this evidence? Is this worth wasting everybody's time? We'll tell her to go see her own physician. But to be honest, I don't think any doctor is going to find anything he'd be okay with putting in a report. No medical findings no police report, no more lost time. But let's say it is true *[Grimaces, in the negative]* then we'll proceed.

Fullerton - *[Fullerton moves toward Rebecca]* Would you come with me for just a second, Miss?

Rebecca - Where are you taking me?

Fullerton - Don't worry... just routine. We have to put everything into the report. This way please.

[Pause. Reilly leaves, chuffing resignedly]

[End of Scene III]

Silence is a barrier that separates more than barbed wire and hurts more than torture

Scene IV - Keller's Office

[Another room. A table, a couch and two chairs. Fullerton and Rebecca enter. Rebecca sits as Fullerton gestures goodbye and leaves Rebecca with officer Keller]

Keller - Good evening, Ms. White. Officer Fullerton's filled me in about your awful experience. I want you to be as calm as you can be, and show me the marks where he hit you.

[Pause. Keller reviews Fullerton's notes]

[Keller's expression tenses as she reads and changes visibly. Silence. The effect of Keller's silence has a noticeable impact on Rebecca, who appears unsettled at Keller's reaction to the notes she is reading]

Rebecca - I'm sorry, Officer. Is something wrong with the notes?

[Pause. Woman enters from the end of the room toward Rebecca]

Woman - What did I tell you? You should have prepared better. This is a woman, not some stupid man. You can't trick this one, Rebecca.

Rebecca - *[Looks upset at Woman then turns to Keller]* Look... Officer... if it's because everything is confused, it's because... I'm still in shock... Yes, I'm shocked. He scared me and... he... threatened to kill my daughter.

[Pause to let this bomb drop]

Woman - Be serious. Your daughter isn't a kid anymore. And she lives 200... 300 miles away? My God... poor Carlo... we're turning him into a mafia "Don".

Rebecca - *[To Keller]* He... He's Italian! He has a lot of problems! He knows shady people in Monterey who will kill for a thousand dollars. He would gladly have Heather killed! He would kill my daughter! I didn't have any money. I wanted to go. I even asked my father to lend me the money. He said he would lend it to me if I reported him! I had to do it. I don't want him to do to anyone else what he did to me. No, he has to pay.

Keller - Don't worry Miss, we'll take a couple of pictures now, then you'll go to a doctor for an exam. Then tell them to get in contact with us.

Woman - *[Leans into Rebecca, in her ear]* Hmm... the 6th of July doesn't work, by the way. It's too recent. Besides, don't you remember? Carlo wasn't even here on the 6th. And if you look at your telephone log, there are too many phone calls. How can you be on the phone and be having your ass kicked at the same time? Don't be ridiculous.

[Fade to black as the Woman and Keller stand above, looking with wan smiles at Rebecca]

[End of Scene IV]

Scene V - Fullerton's Office

[Office of Fullerton. One day later. Passage of time is evident by folders and picture gathered on the desk. Reilly is passing pictures to Fullerton one at a time]

Reilly - I went to the apartment where she said it happened. Neat as a pin. Nothing out of the ordinary. Sound logical to you? Officer Keller says the only physical evidence is a little, faded bruise on the right arm...

Fullerton - Looks like we're dealing with Wonder Woman.

Reilly - Come on, Mark, be serious. Here's how I had to write it up: "After White was tied up, Parlanti told White that he wanted to make love to her. White did not say anything. Parlanti tried to 'make love' to White but she did not respond. White told Parlanti that she was hurting and she did not want to do this. I asked White if Parlanti actually inserted his penis into her vagina. White said 'Yes'. I asked White how long Parlanti's penis was in her vagina. White estimated three to four minutes. I asked White if Parlanti ejaculated. White said, 'No, he doesn't do that'. White explained that Parlanti never ejaculates. I asked White if Parlanti maintained an erection during the entire time. White said, 'Yes'. I asked White how many times she told Parlanti to stop. White said, 'At least twice'. I asked White if he stopped right away. White said, 'No. He gave up because I wasn't responding to him and he was angered'. White then passed out or went to sleep. Parlanti left the room and went back to his office."

Does it sound plausible? Is this going to make us a laughingstock?

Fullerton - John, look at it this way: no doctor is going to issue a report for something that never happened. And if they do, it's not our problem anyway.

[Phone rings. Fullerton answers]

Fullerton - Sheriff's office, Fullerton.

[A female voice on the caller's end is heard]

Voice Off - Yes. This is Ms. White. I wanted to call and tell you... I was looking at my calendar and wanted to let you know... what I told you, that's all correct, but it's shifted one week. It wasn't July the 6th but June 29th... The days of the week are the same, but the dates are different.

Fullerton - Thank you, Miss. I'm going to add it to the report. I'm still hoping to hear from you as soon as you find a doctor to see you.
[Ends the call]

Reilly - This is against regs, Mark. We should have taken her to the doctor ourselves.

Fullerton - Don't worry, even if she gets a doctor, it's all going to resolve. She's American, he's Italian... need I say more?

[End of Scene V]

Silence is a barrier that separates more than barbed wire and hurts more than torture

Scene VI - Fullerton's Office

[One week later, same room, same characters]

Fullerton - Okay. Here's the last of it. Give it your okay and we can close the report:

"On 7/20/2002, White paged me and I called her back. White told me that she spent a few hours today looking at a calendar and figuring dates. White told me that the days of the week were accurate, but the actual incident occurred on Saturday, June 29th, 2002. The week she described to me ended on Monday, July 8th, 2002. Parlanti was home with White until he left for his business trip on Tuesday, July 16th, 2002. Nothing of significance occurred during that week except for 'verbal abuse' by Parlanti. White told me that she was writing out the incident on a computer. I asked White if she was sure about the dates. White reviewed the dates with me again over the phone while she had access to a calendar. White was sure that the incident started on June 29th, 2002. I gave White the fax number to the East County Detective's Bureau and told her to fax her written report to me on Monday, July 22nd, 2002. On July 22nd, 2002, I received the faxed copy of White's account of the incident. White called me and told me that she was going to see a doctor today because her ribs were still hurting from Parlanti's kicks. I asked White to have the doctor's office fax me a copy of her medical report. Later that same day, I received a copy of Dr. Troy Manchester's report. Dr. Manchester noted fractures to White's sixth and seventh ribs. On 8/1/2002, Dr. Manchester called me back and I spoke with him about White's injuries. I asked Dr. Manchester if he was able to determine the date that White obtained the injuries to her ribs. Dr. Manchester said that he could not pinpoint an exact date, but he was sure that the injuries occurred within a month of White's visit on July 22nd, 2002.

On 7/30/2002, I received a follow-up report authored by Deputy Fullerton. Deputy Fullerton contacted a maintenance worker who was employed at the apartment complex that White lived at. (W-l) Alfred Berger told Deputy Fullerton that he saw White limping, but he was unsure if she had any facial injuries. Berger was unsure because White was wearing sunglasses. Refer to Deputy Fullerton's report for further information. Based on the above information, Sgt. Flannigan and I determined that there was probable cause to arrest Parlanti for the above listed charges. On 7/31/2002 and 8/1/2002, I made several unsuccessful attempts to arrest Parlanti at his home and work."

Reilly - That's the most absurd thing I've ever heard. I asked her for evidence, photographs, anything. She had nothing. But I guess if the D.A. wants this so bad, that's their business. If they're so hot to kill "Romeo", nobody's going to look into the particulars.

[Fade to black]

[End of Scene VI]

Silence is a barrier that separates more than barbed wire and hurts more than torture

Scene VII - Katia's Apartment

[A few seconds in the dark. Lights up on a small couch center stage on which a girl sits next to a reporter, who holds out a small micro-recorder toward her.]

Reporter - Ms. Anedda. The story of Mr. Parlanti is... I'm sorry... "surreal". You're considered his long standing girlfriend. Can you give us a comment? What caused you to become so convinced of his innocence?

Katia - You know, because of the arrest, we were actually out of touch for several days. I was under the impression that he was working in Germany, to be honest. After getting over the shock of his arrest, I started gathering all the information I could about what had happened. All I had to do was read the report issued by the Ventura County Sheriff's Department to realize the obvious unreliability of both the facts and the accuser. *[Shuffles out a paper to the journalist]* A journalist from the newspaper... "La Nazione", who's written about this story, has called the police report a "substitute, produced by the fertile mind of an American soap opera play-writer". I'm in love with Carlo, and this story has destroyed my dream of a life together with him. It also drained us all financially, his friends, his family, myself... but please believe me. This is not the main reason I have fought so hard for 6 years to make at least one voice in his defense be heard. I've been sitting in a courtroom in Ventura, for four days, listening to a woman telling stories that were physically and biologically impossible. Those same stories today are declared impossible by experts. I listened as she invented lie after lie, dozens of lies. These lies were readily disproven as perjuries, from her own admission, from the defense attorney's questioning... even from the questioning of the District Attorney! And then... countless stories... all contradictory to each other. So many, in fact, the defense attorney nick-named her "the consistently inconsistent Rebecca White." For 10 days I listened to a prosecutor describe the "Italian" nature of the defendant. Here is an excerpt from his closing arguments:

"Now, 85 percent of batterers are male, and the reason why they batter is because they have that need to exert that power and control over their significant others. The defendant, very clear, fancies himself a Romeo. He likes to go out and meet women. He likes to talk to women. He likes the way women make him feel. There was no doubt about that in this trial". This is just another way of saying DEATH TO ROMEO"; this is what is made plain by reading the trial transcripts.

For the last 6 years I've had to watch powerlessly as every fundamental human right of Carlo's was violated. And after getting information online, I discovered that what is happening to Carlo is, in fact, in many ways, a social illness... a dangerous one... that damages, in first analysis, the real victims of violence

[Takes out another paper from her large sheaf of documents]

I want to read to you the enlightening ending of an article that Karen Stephenson has written for Rolling Stone Magazine:

Women Are Victims Too

"Men are not the only victims of women who make false allegations. Women who are the real victims of rape, are further victimized by those who make false accusations. Words and actions by a false accuser rob the real-life victims of rape of badly needed services. These women abuse police, prosecutors and victim group resources, taking time, money and resources away from those who truly need and deserve help.

The Need for Justice

Although legislative amendment is needed, it cannot immediately stop the frequency of false allegations of rape. Society needs strict laws to aid in the education process that no one has the right to make a false allegation.

Rape is an appalling crime. False accusations of rape and the lack of accountability should be just as intolerable a crime as physical rape itself."

You see? The entire story could be played as a perfect farce, were it not for the tragedy it has caused in Carlo's life and in the lives of so many innocent people to come.

[Curtain]

[As the curtain descends a voice off: Carlo Parlanti begins. Even in the English version, the Italian of Carlo should be played, for the sake of conveying the authenticity of this vignette. It is voiced over with an American English version after 4 or 5 words.]

Carlo - I'm Carlo Parlanti, and I'm talking to you from Avenal State Prison, a concentration camp in the California desert.

I've already been imprisoned for six years, yet in all that time I have never once stopped proclaiming my innocence or fighting for the truth.

During the farce of a trial I received, my accuser had already been caught flagrantly committing perjury, but, sadly, the logic of lynching has prevailed.

However, since then the truth has inexorably surfaced: fake pictures, concealed evidence, manufactured documents … A vicious circle that, in order to cover the stupid mistakes of a couple of cops and one District Attorney, has become a conspiracy to obstruct justice and commit crimes.

In the past two years these droplets of evidence have become a deluge. There are now a dozen doctors and criminologists who are attesting that the "facts" attributed to me are not even possible from a physical or medical point of view!

Some of these experts are so outraged that they are filing criminal charges right here in the United States, where corrupt physicians have created from scratch injuries such as ecchymosis and skull fractures! Unfortunately for them, there are photographs from the police, medical certificates and even MRIs disavowing their claims (all of which were already in the hands of the District Attorney's Office itself, but never produced at trial).

But this outrage reached new heights of absurdity with Dr. Pugach, who has abetted my accuser to appear disabled by concealing all the tests and exams performed on her by himself and by penning a letter that deserves to be in the annals of medical malpractice!

I'm not appealing to your good heart, but instead to your intelligence: the police have withheld evidence; the District Attorney has introduced false evidence in a court of law; the doctors (assuming they can be called by that title) have signed false certificates and one of them has even stolen money from the Social Security Administration…

They are the criminals. Don't let them get away with this.

[End of Scene VII]

[Finish]

APPENDICES

Act one – Scene I – A living Room

Carlo Parlanti's living room, in perfect order

Scene IV - Keller's Office

Rebecca White
at the Police station

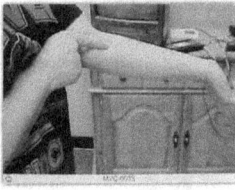

Her arm, where she claimed
being bitten

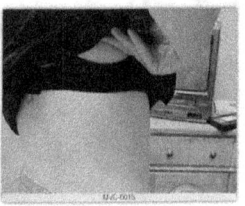

Her back, where she reported
being kicked dozens of times

Silence is a barrier that separates more than barbed wire and hurts more than torture

Scene VI – Fullerton's Office

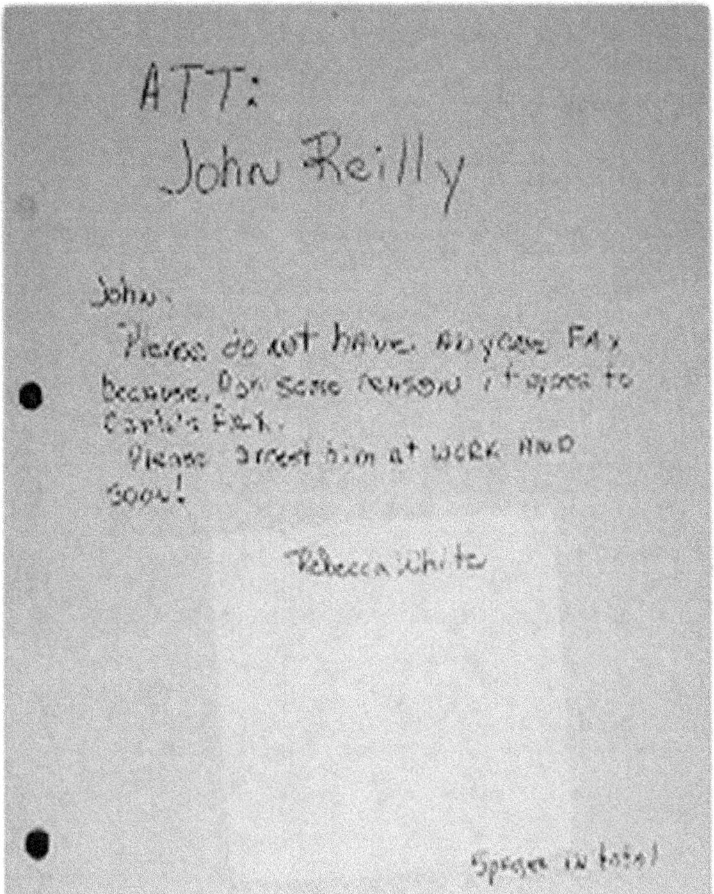

Fax sent from Rebecca White to Deputy Reilly

			1 R.D.	2 BEAT	3 RB NUMBER
			9150	9G	02-54174

4 CODE	5 ITEM	6 QTY	7 ITEM NAME	8 BRAND / MAKE MANUFACTURER	9 MODEL NAME OR NUMBER	10 MISC. DESCRIPTION	11 IDENTIFICATION / SERIAL NUMBER	12 VALUE

☒ Supplemental   ☐ Case Cleared

☐ Gang   ☒ Domestic   ☐ Hate   ☐ Child Abuse   ☐ Elderly Abuse

Connecting Report Numbers:

Code Section / Description: 273.5 P.C. / Domestic Battery / 261 P.C. / Rape / 236 P.C. / False Imprisonment

Code: (V)   Name: White, Rebecca McKay

On 07-19-02, I interviewed Kevin Bunch at his residence. I asked Bunch to call me if he saw White. At approximately 1730 hours, Bunch paged me and told me White was at her residence "moving out." I drove over to White's location with Sgt. Flannigan. White had already left but I noticed her vehicle in front of her apartment. I waited approximately one hour and White did not show up. I left a business card on White's vehicle asking her to call me before she left town. At approximately 1915 hours, White paged me stating that she was already on her way out of town. White was near the Civic Arts Center on Thousand Oaks Blvd. I called White and arranged to meet her at the Civic Arts Center in Thousand Oaks. I meet White at approximately 2000 hours. I interviewed White with Deputy Lanquist #4105 as a witness. The interview took place in my Detective car with White in the passenger seat and Deputy Lanquist in the backseat.

STATEMENT OF (V) REBECCA WHITE

The following is a synopsis of my tape-recorded interview with White. White has been dating (S) Carlo Parlanti for the last year and a half and they have been living together for the last nine months. On Saturday, July 6th, Parlanti was stressed out because White's mother and daughter had been in town for a visit. White's mother and daughter left on the same day at approximately 1800 hours. Parlanti was also having problems with a computer program that he was working on. Parlanti drank a two-litter bottle of wine and asked White to go buy him more wine. White left the residence and

000027

13 DATE / TIME OF REPORT	14 REPORTING OFFICER / ID NO / DIV / UNIT	15 APPROVED BY ID / LD NO
08/02/02 / 09:55	J. Reilly #2988 / ECPS / DETS	W. ___ , SGT# 1225

REV 3/92   NARRCONV/HPT

Rebecca White's statement

			1 H.O.	2 BEAT	3 RB NUMBER
			9150	2G	02-54174

4 CODE	5 ITEM	6 QTY	7 ITEM NAME	8 BRAND / MAKE MANUFACTURER	9 MODEL NAME OR NUMBER	10 MISC. DESCRIPTION	11 IDENTIFICATION / SERIAL NUMBER	12 VALUE

bought another two-liter bottle of wine. When White returned home from the store, Parlanti was already angry. Parlanti started drinking the second bottle of wine and told White to get out of his sight. White thought that he meant for her to get out of the room. White went into the bedroom. I asked White if she always does what Parlanti tells her to do. White said, "Yes, especially when he's drinking." Parlanti has been violent with White in the past, but the violence only occurs when Parlanti consumes alcohol.

White was in bed when Parlanti entered the room approximately ten minutes later. Parlanti told White he wanted her to leave his apartment. White said that she would leave and started to get dressed. As White was getting dressed, Parlanti became angry because she was going to leave. Parlanti grabbed White and banged her head against the bulletin board that was by the front door. White had "knots" on her head as a result of Parlanti banging her head. Parlanti then "threw" White to the adjacent wall and began to slap her. White estimated that Parlanti slapped her ten times. White's left eye began to swell shut. White started to shake in fear because he had never been this violent in the past. White told Parlanti that she wanted to leave. Parlanti said that he didn't want her to leave. Parlanti then started "choking" White. White said that her neck was still swollen the next day. White then lost consciousness and fell to the floor.

When White regained consciousness, she was lying on her abdomen. Parlanti was on White's right side with his left knee in her back. Parlanti was still chocking White. White described the position as a "chokehold." White again passed out. When White regained consciousness, she was "on the other side of the room on the floor. He was kicking me on my right ribs." White was screaming and she described the kicks as "really hard." White "rolled up in a ball" and told Parlanti that he was hurting her. Parlanti started kicking White again. White "blacked out" again and started screaming even louder. Parlanti kicked White again and told her that she was trying to get him in trouble by her screaming. White was having troubles breathing because of the kicks to the right side of her body. White said, "I could barely talk because he hit me so hard on my jaw." The soreness to White's jaw occurred when Parlanti was slapping her near the front door.

Parlanti then grabbed White by her left arm and drug her to a beanbag chair that was in the living room. White told Parlanti that she was having problems seeing.

000028

13 DATE / TIME OF REPORT	14 REPORTING OFFICER / ID NO / DIV / UNIT	15 APPROVING / ID NO
08/02/02 / 09:55	J. Reilly #2988 / ECPS / DETS	W. ___ 5674 1225

1 R.D.	2 BEAT	3 RB NUMBER
9150	9G	02-54174

4 CODE	5 ITEM	6 QTY	7 ITEM NAME	8 BRAND / MAKE MANUFACTURER	9 MODEL NAME OR NUMBER	10 MISC. DESCRIPTION	11 IDENTIFICATION / SERIAL NUMBER	12 VALUE

Parlanti grabbed White by the hair and drug her down the hall into the office. Parlanti picked White up and made her sit on the coach in the office. Parlanti again told White that she was not leaving. Parlanti said that he didn't know what to do with her now because he knew that he hurt her and she would call the police. Parlanti then brought out the telephone and told White to call "911" so he could "finish this off." White knew that if she touched the phone Parlanti would hit her again. White said, "I was hurting so bad, I didn't want him to hit me anymore." White tried to get up but she was having problems breathing because of the injuries to her ribs.

Parlanti then went on his computer (that was in the office) and pulled up a website of women being tied up. Parlanti told White that he wanted her to pick out the way that he was going to tie her up. Parlanti has tied White up during prior beatings so she was afraid. White again asked to leave but Parlanti would not allow her to. Parlanti then "dragged" White by her left arm into the bedroom. He then removed all of White's clothing. Parlanti went and retrieved some "plastic strappings" that were in the hall closet. I asked White if the plastic strappings were still there. White said, "Yes." Parlanti then put one "plastic strap" on each of White's wrists and ankles. Parlanti pulled the straps as tight as he could make them. Parlanti tied White's right arm to her right ankle and her left arm to her left ankle.

After White was tied up, Parlanti told White that he wanted to make love to her. White did not say anything. Parlanti tried to "make love" to White but she did not respond. White told Parlanti that she was hurting and she did not want to do this. I asked White if Parlanti actually inserted his penis into her vagina. White said, "Yes." I asked White how long Parlanti's penis was in her vagina. White estimated three to four minutes. I asked White if Parlanti ejaculated. White said, "No, he doesn't do that." White explained that Parlanti never ejaculates. I asked White if Parlanti maintained an erection during the entire time. White said, "Yes." I asked White how many times she told Parlanti to stop. White said, "At least twice." I asked White if he stopped right away. White said, "No, he gave up because I wasn't responding to him and he was angered." White then passed out or went to sleep. Parlanti left the room and went back to his office.

White "came to" and yelled to Parlanti. White asked Parlanti to take the straps off of her hands because they were turning purple and were hurting her. Parlanti said that he would not untie her because she was a woman and she would report him. Parlanti

000029

13 DATE / TIME OF REPORT	14 REPORTING OFFICER I D NO / DIV / UNIT	15 APPROVED BY I D NO
08/02/02 / 09-55	J. Reilly #2986 / ECPS / DETS	W. Flanagan SGT #1225
REV 9/97		HARRODIAWHIT

1 H.D.	2 BEAT	3 R8 NUMBER
9150	9G	02-54174

4 CODE	5 ITEM	6 QTY	7 ITEM NAME	8 BRAND / MAKE MANUFACTURER	9 MODEL NAME OR NUMBER	10 MISC. DESCRIPTION	11 IDENTIFICATION / SERIAL NUMBER	12 VALUE

urned the light on and noticed that White's wrists were swollen. He then cut the straps off of White's wrist. Parlanti then tied White up again but the ties were not as tight. Parlanti tied White up the same way, right wrist to right ankle and left wrist to left ankle. Parlanti then left the room. White passed out again.

When White "came to," her wrists were still swollen and she was "hurting." White started yelling to Parlanti. Parlanti told White to shut up because he thought the neighbors would call the police. Parlanti then cut off the straps off White's wrists and ankles. Parlanti then said that he wanted to "make love" to White. White said, "Carlo, I don't want to make love to you. I'm hurting too bad, please don't." I asked White if she physically tried to resist him. White said, "I'm hurting too bad, no." Parlanti's penis entered White's vagina. I asked White how long this occurred. White said, "It was longer than last time because he was determined." Parlanti said, "I'm going to make you feel better because I know that I hurt you and then I'm going to take you to a motel room in the morning and I don't want you in my life anymore." White said, "You can't make me feel any better Carlo, you've hurt me and I'm hurting really bad, please stop." I asked White what made him stop. White said, "I'm not responding, I mean if I'm not responding he's not getting anything out of it." White asked Parlanti for some pain medicine. Parlanti brought White back an unknown type of pain medicine.

Parlanti told White that he needed to get some sleep. Parlanti "handcuffed" White to him with the strappings. White's left wrist was tied to Parlanti's right wrist. Parlanti told White that she had to make love to him a third time. Parlanti told White to get on top of him. White said, "I can't, Carlo I'm hurting, I know you broke my ribs, you've done something to me really bad." Parlanti said that he didn't care and White was going to do what he wanted. Parlanti then laid down on top of White. White said, "I couldn't move, I hurt too bad." Parlanti then became angry and threw White off of him. White was still handcuffed to Parlanti. They were lying side by side. Parlanti and White then went to sleep. White estimated that she was first tied up between 2400 hours and 0030 hours. The last time she was tied up was between 0200 hours and 0300 hours.

The next thing White remembered was the alarm clock going off at 0630 hours. White could not open her eyes but she felt that Parlanti was no longer tied to her. Parlanti tried to wake White up. White remembered Parlanti touching her and hearing his voice, but she could not wake up. White told Parlanti to leave her alone because

000030

---

1 R.D.	2 BEAT	3 RB NUMBER
9150	9G	02-54174

4 CODE	5 ITEM	6 QTY	7 ITEM NAME	8 BRAND / MAKE MANUFACTURER	9 MODEL NAME OR NUMBER	10 MISC. DESCRIPTION	11 IDENTIFICATION / SERIAL NUMBER	12 VALUE

he was still hurting. Parlanti turned White over and saw that her face was "black" and her throat was swollen. Parlanti said that White was not leaving the apartment looking like that. Parlanti then put some "Ben Gay" and put it on all of White's bruises except her face because it burned. The "Ben Gay" was a special kind that he had previously bought to put on White's prior injuries. Parlanti then packed White's head and throat in bags of ice. White could not open her mouth to take the pain medication so Parlanti put them in her mouth and gave her a straw to drink some water. White did not remember anything throughout the rest of the day except Parlanti waking her up to see if she was "ok."

That night, Parlanti again tied White back to him. Nothing happened during the course of the night. On Monday, White remembered the alarm going off at 0630 hours. White heard Parlanti saying to himself, "Oh my gosh, what have I done to her" because White had swelled even more. Parlanti did not know what to do. He then cut the strap off of White's wrist and put more "Ben Gay" on her. Parlanti then gave White more pain medicine. White did not think that Parlanti went to work that day, but she was not sure because she did not get out of bed. Parlanti again tied White to him before he went to sleep.

On Tuesday morning, White woke up when the alarm went off a 0630 hours. Parlanti told White that she needed to get up and use the restroom and make him coffee. White got out of bed and coffee. Parlanti left for work and White went back to bed. I asked White why she didn't call the police. White paused and then said, "Because I would be in greater danger." White said that she didn't call the police because Parlanti would have her and her daughter killed. Parlanti told White in the past that a "hitman" was going to kill her and her daughter. White called her mother and daughter and told them that she had fallen down a flight of stairs and she was injured.

At approximately 1400 hours, Parlanti came home from work with food. He told White that she needed to get up and eat. Parlanti also told White that he was going to help her take a bath because she "stunk." Parlanti helped White take a shower. White's hair came out when she was washing it. White was scarred because so much of hair fell out that it clogged the drain. White described Parlanti as an "angel" that day. White said, "He was very gentle." On Tuesday night, Parlanti tied White to his wrist again before they went to sleep. I asked White if she thought that it was strange

000031

---

					1 R.O.	2 BEAT	3 RB NUMBER
					9150	9G	02-54174
4 CODE	5 ITEM	6 QTY	7 ITEM NAME	8 BRAND / MAKE MANUFACTURER	9 MODEL NAME OR NUMBER	10 MISC. DESCRIPTION	11 IDENTIFICATION / SERIAL NUMBER	12 VALUE

or Parlanti to tie her up at night, but not during the day when he was gone for work. White said that her ex-husband tried to kill her and she learned not to fight back because she would lose. I again asked White why she couldn't leave. White said that she couldn't walk because it hurt. I told White that she was able to get up and make coffee, why couldn't she leave when he was gone for the day. White said, "There's three reasons. Number one was that she promised him she wouldn't. Number two, White knew that Parlanti would hurt her and her daughter. Number three was that she did not want Parlanti to be hurt anymore. White later told me that she didn't want to report this incident but her father said that he would not help her unless she helped herself and reported the crime to the police.

Parlanti again handcuffed White to him when they went to bed for the night. The next day, Wednesday, Parlanti told White that she needed to do some things beside sleep. Parlanti told White to do the laundry and take another shower by herself. The only time White left the apartment was to do the laundry. White met a Hispanic female on the sidewalk. The female saw White's injuries and asked what happened. White told the female that she fell down some stairs and she might have broken her ribs. The female told White her apartment number and offered to help White if she needed it. White finished the laundry and went back to her apartment. Parlanti returned home rom work and brought White some "gifts."

Later that night, White had sexual intercourse with Parlanti. White explained that the sexual intercourse was consensual and she was a willing participant. I asked White why she would have sexual intercourse with Parlanti. White said, "I love Carlo, whether he hurt me or not doesn't matter." I told White that I didn't think that Parlanti was holding her against her will the whole time. White said, "Not during the day, no." I asked White if Parlanti tied her up again after they had intercourse. White said, "Yes." White thinks that Parlanti tied her up because he thought that she was going to hurt him.

On Thursday morning, Parlanti woke up and went to work. Parlanti got home from work and nothing of significance happened. When they went to bed, Parlanti again tied White to him. Parlanti woke up on Friday and went to work. Parlanti got home from work at approximately 1700 hours and started drinking wine. White explained that Parlanti would come home from work and drink a two-litter bottle of wine. White said, "That started his drinking binge, the night he beat me up." Nothing of significance

000032

13 DATE / TIME OF REPORT	14 REPORTING OFFICER / ID NO / ORI / UNIT	15 APPROVED BY / ID NO
08/02/02 / 00:55	J. Reilly #2088 / ECPS / DETS	W. Flagg, SGT #1225
REV 8/97		NARCCOMP KIT

4 CODE	5 ITEM	6 QTY	7 ITEM NAME	8 BRAND / MAKE MANUFACTURER	9 MODEL NAME OR NUMBER	10 MISC. DESCRIPTION	11 IDENTIFICATION / SERIAL NUMBER	12 VALUE

occurred on Friday night. On Friday, White had to sleep on the couch because she "didn't deserve to sleep with him."

On Saturday, Parlanti was home all day with White. Parlanti was working on his computer. Nothing of significance occurred on Saturday. On Sunday, White told Parlanti that her ribs were still hurting. Parlanti told White that he wasn't going to drink anymore because he didn't want to hurt her anymore. On Monday, nothing of significance occurred. On Tuesday at approximately 0400 hours, Parlanti left town for a business trip. On 07-18-02, White drove to the Sheriff Station and reported the crimes. I asked White why she waited so long to report the incident. White said that she couldn't drive. I asked White why she didn't call us. White said that the phone has a recorder on it. Parlanti told White before he left for his business trip that everything White says and does Parlanti would know about. White finally came to the police station to report the incident because she spoke to her father who would not help her unless she reported the incident to the police.

I asked White if the ties that Parlanti used to tie her up were still at the apartment. White said that Parlanti disposed of the ties that he used on her every morning but the unused ties were still there. I asked White if we could go to the apartment and retrieve the ties. White agreed to go back to the apartment.

END OF INTERVIEW

Deputy Lanquist and I drove White to her apartment. White opened the closet and I retrieved a bag of plastic ties. White walked through the apartment with me and showed me where the various locations where the crimes occurred. I photographed the apartment and the locations inside of the apartment that she pointed out to me. I booked the film and the ties into evidence at the East County Property Room. White was leaving town so she left me phone numbers that I could contact her at. White also told me that she was going to see a doctor within the next couple of days.

On 07-20-02, White paged me and I called her back. White told me that she spent a few hours today looking at a calendar and figuring dates. White told me that the days of the week were accurate, but the actual incident occurred on Saturday June 29, 2002. The week she described to me ended on Monday July 8, 2002. Parlanti was home with White until he left for his business trip on Tuesday, July 16, 2002. Nothing

000033

13 DATE / TIME OF REPORT	14 REPORTING OFFICER / ID NO / DIV / UNIT	15 APPROVED / VALID NO
08/02/02 / 09:55	J. Reilly #2988 / ECPS / DETS	W. ... SBT#1285

						1 R.D.	2 BEAT	3 RB NUMBER
						9150	9G	02-54174
CODE	ITEM	QTY	7 ITEM NAME	8 BRAND / MAKE MANUFACTURER	9 MODEL NAME OR NUMBER	10 MISC. DESCRIPTION	11 IDENTIFICATION / SERIAL NUMBER	12 VAL

of significance occurred during that week except for "verbal abuse" by Parlanti. White told me that she was writing out the incident on a computer. I asked White if she was sure about the dates. White reviewed the dates with me again over the phone while she had access to a calendar. White was sure that the incident started on June 29, 2002. I gave White the fax number to the East County Detective Bureau and told her to fax her written report to me on Monday, July 22, 2002.

On July 22, 2002, I received the faxed copy of White's account of the incident. White called me and told me that she was going to see a doctor today because her rib were still hurting from Parlanti's kicks. I asked White to have the doctor's office fax me a copy of her medical report. Later that same day, I received a faxed copy of Dr. Troy _____. Dr. Manchester noted fractures to White's sixth and seventh ribs. On 08-01-02, Dr. Manchester called me back and I spoke with him about White's injuries. I asked Dr. Manchester if he was able to determine the date that White obtained the injuries to her ribs. Dr. Manchester said that he could not pinpoint an exact date, but he was sure that the injuries occurred within a month of White's visit on July 22, 2002.

On 07-30-02, I received a follow-up report authored by Deputy Fullerton. Deputy Fullerton contacted a maintenance worker who was employed at the apartment complex that White lived at. (W-1) Alfred Berger told Deputy Fullerton that he saw White limping, but he was unsure if she had any facial injuries. Berger was unsure because White was wearing sunglasses. Refer to Deputy Fullerton's report for further information.

Based on the above information, Sgt. Flannigan and I determined that there was probable cause to arrest Parlanti for the above listed charges. On 07-31-02 and 08-01-02, I made several unsuccessful attempts to arrest Parlanti at his home and work.

000034

13 DATE / TIME OF REPORT	14 REPORTING OFFICER / ID NO / DIV / UNIT	15 APPROVED BY / ID NO
08-02-02 / 09:55	J. Reilly #2988 / ECPS / DETS	W. 7___ 16th/2005

Skin...	Intact, Warm, Dry, No visible rash or remarkable lesion
Eyes...	PERRLA, EOMI, Sclera white and clear
Ears...	
Left Ear...	External Auditory Canal Clear, Non-Erythematous, TM Pearly Gray. Landmarks and Light Reflexes Present
Right Ear...	External Auditory Canal Clear, Non-Erythematous, TM Pearly Gray. Landmarks and Light Reflexes Present
Nose...	Nares patent, No drainage
Mouth / Pharynx...	No oral lesions, Pharynx non-injected, without exudate
Head...	Atraumatic
Neck...	Supple, No lymphadenopathy, No thyromegaly
Cardiovascular...	Regular Rate, Regular Rhythm, No Significant Murmur Noted
Chest...	Symmetrical respiratory effort, No retractions, Clear to auscultation, No dullness to percussion, Good air exchange, Normal I:E ratio, No signs of consolidation or effusion
Musculoskeletal...	Muscle strength normal bilaterally. Tone normal, Gait normal, Focused exams
Focused exams...	
Joints...	Back
Back...	
Appearance...	No redness, No edema, No bruising, No visible deformity
Exam...	No warmth, No palpable deformity, Normal ROM, Tenderness
Tenderness...	
Location	Right lateral, Thoracic, Lumbar, Sacral
Functional assessment...	Normal reflexes, Normal sensation, Normal muscle strength
Neurologic...	Alert and oriented x4 with proper affect, Motor function normal

ASSESSMENT

922.31   Contusion Of Back

Unfortunate Victim of recurrent and severe domestic violence.
Police from home region have delayed filing a claim for unclear reasons, I am
concerned regarding her safety. Pt is here with her daughter, but the alleged
attacker is from the area.
Instructed patient to contact the officer she contacted in her home town, and
also in Monterey.
Safety discussed.
Right rib fractures and soft tissue injury, post traumatic anxiety.
Using anti-inflammatories and ultram for pain.
education.

000658

Extract from Dr. Manchester's report

*"Few hundreds' criminals may also be released into liberty,
but not even one innocent must end up in prison,
because this would transform
the entire legal system into a criminal system"
(Venkatraman Iyer)*

An Act of Civility

Donate a smile to a prisoner – support Prisoners of Silence

http://www.PrisonersOfSilence.org

paypal sostieni@prigionieridelsilenzio.it

support Prisoners of Silence

Bank Carife: Iban: IT78E0615501600000000001447 bac SWIFT CFERIT2F

Standard support level: $20

Premium support level: $150

*Carlo could be you,
Carlo could be your son,
Carlo could be your best friend
That picked you up in the darkest days of your life.
Pretending that nothing is going on means
Being an accomplice to the pain and to
The crime that will keep repeating itself*

Silence is a barrier that separates more than barbed wire and hurts more than torture

Front cover drawing by: *Israel Gowan*

*"They removed her blindfold
so that she had to see the truth,
they gagged her mouth
so that she could not reveal it."*

Carlo Parlanti

Back cover drawing of Katia Anedda by: *Richard Arciniega*

Silence is a barrier that separates more than barbed wire and hurts more than torture

PERSONAL NOTES:

Silence is a barrier that separates more than barbed wire and hurts more than torture

----

Silence is a barrier that separates more than barbed wire and hurts more than torture

----

Silence is a barrier that separates more than barbed wire and hurts more than torture

---

Silence is a barrier that separates more than barbed wire and hurts more than torture

www.ingramcontent.com/pod-product-compliance
Lightning Source LLC
Chambersburg PA
CBHW051927220626
47052CB00003B/606